The Mouth with a Mind of Its Own

by Patricia L. Mervine, M.A., CCC-SLP

Illustrated by Nayan Soni

About the Author: Pat Mervine is a speech/language pathologist, assistive technology consultant, and children's book author. She has been working to improve the communication skills of children like Matthew for over 20 years. Pat is the creator of the popular web site, www.speakingofspeech.com, and the blog, www.speakingofspeech.blog.com, two tremendous resources for SLPs, teachers, parents, and other who support children who have communication impairments.

You can learn more about Pat and her books at her author site, www.patmervine.com.

Other books by Pat Mervine, available through www.patmervine.com:

How Katie Got a Voice (and a cool new nickname)

There Was a Speech Teacher Who Swallowed Some Dice

Note: While this book accurately describes the process of speech therapy,

it is a work of fiction and all characters in the story are fictional.

ISBN-13: 978-0692202319 (Speaking of Speech.com., Inc.)

DEDICATION

To SLPs everywhere who, with endless patience, encouragement, and creativity,
tame wild mouths every day!
Each child you help is like a pebble in a pond…the ripple effect of your work lasts a lifetime.

Matthew had a problem with his mouth. Oh, it worked well enough when he ate and drank and chewed bubble gum. But when he tried to talk, his mouth simply wouldn't cooperate. When he was little, everyone thought his baby talk was cute. Now that he was in school, Matthew didn't think it was cute, not one little bit.

On the first day of school,
the teacher greeted each student.
"What is your name?"
she asked Matthew.

"Matthew," he thought, but
"Mah-yoo," said his mouth.

"Mah Who?" asked the teacher.
"Mah-yoo!" said his mouth.

Matthew
Matthew

Mah-yoo
Mah-yoo

"Well, Mah Yoo, I don't seem
to have you on my list. No
problem, take a seat and we'll
figure this out later."
Matthew shrugged his
shoulders and sat down.

Sadly, things didn't get any better at snack. "What do you want to eat?" asked the teacher. "A cookie, please," he thought. "Too - ee peze," said his mouth.

"Two peas? Sorry, Mah, we don't have peas today, just cookies and chips. Which would you like?"

"Chips," he thought, but "Sits," said his mouth. "Okay, Mah, you can just sit," replied the teacher. And so Matthew sat glumly through snack without anything to eat or drink.

A cookie please

Too-ee peze

When the bell rang, Matthew ran outside for recess, hoping to make some new friends. He walked over to a group of kids on the playground. "What do you want to do, Mah?" asked a girl from his class. Matthew thought, "Let's slide!" but his mouth said "Wet hi." "Say what?" asked the girl. "Want to play tag?" thought Matthew, but "wannoopaytad?" said his mouth. "I don't think Mah speaks English," the girl whispered to the other kids, and they ran off to play, leaving Matthew behind.

Matthew never felt so alone. At home, his family understood him when he talked….well, most of the time, anyway. But here in school, nobody understood anything he said. He couldn't even make them understand his name! How humiliating.

When the students went back into the classroom, the teacher noticed Matthew's long face. "Didn't you have fun at recess, Mah?" she asked. Matthew wanted to yell "MY NAME IS MATTHEW!", but he was so frustrated, all his mouth could say was "ARRRGGGHHH!!!" Matthew sat in silence for the rest of the day.

The next morning when Matthew walked into his classroom, his teacher stopped him at the door. "Good morning, Matthew," she smiled. "I have a friend who wants to meet you." She led Matthew down the hall to a small room next to the nurse's office. "When I figured out that your name is not Mah Yoo, but Matthew, I realized that you had a little problem with your speech," explained his teacher. "My friend, Mrs. Hicks, is a speech and language therapist. I think she will be a big help to you."

Mrs. Hicks chatted with Matthew, asked him to name a bunch of pictures, had him wiggle his tongue all around, and took a lot of notes. Then she smiled.

"Matthew, you are a great kid, but your mouth has a mind of its own. Don't worry, though. Together, we can tame that mouth of yours and everyone will understand you. I will have a meeting with your parents and, in a few weeks, we will start working together."

She handed Matthew a book that had the alphabet and lots of other pages full of pictures arranged in categories, like foods, playground equipment, colors, shapes, and activities. "Until we get your mouth under control, just point to the picture that you are talking about, and your friends will understand." On the cover of the book, Mrs. Hicks wrote in big letters: MY NAME IS MATTHEW.

"Thank you!" thought Matthew, but his mouth said," Fan-noo!"

"You're welcome," said Mrs. Hicks. At last, somebody in the school understood him!

Thank you!

Fan-noo!

MY NAME IS MATTHEW

The picture book was very helpful to Matthew. With it, he could answer questions in class, choose his snack, and play with his classmates at recess. But Matthew couldn't wait to start "taming his mouth" with Mrs. Hicks, although he was a little worried about what that meant.

Twice a week, Matthew went to the speech room, and quickly found that speech therapy was a lot of fun. First, they played a lot of listening games. Mrs. Hicks told Matthew to give a "thumbs up" when she said a speech sound, like /s/ , and then tried to trick him by mixing in other sounds. When he got pretty good at this, she made the game even trickier by covering her mouth. In the beginning, this was really hard, because /f/ and /s/ and /th/ sounded a lot alike to him. With practice, Matthew was winning this game, week after week.

On a "listening train" picture, Matthew had to point to the engine, boxcar, or caboose to show if he heard a speech sound in the beginning, middle, or end of a word. When Matthew first played this game, the sounds seemed all jumbled up, but it wasn't long before he was able to sort them out.

"Now that your ears are tuned up, it's time to tame that mouth," declared Mrs. Hicks.   She explained how the "speech helpers" -- the lips, teeth, tongue, jaw, vocal folds, back of the throat, and lungs -- are all controlled by signals from the brain. When the speech helpers get good signals, they produce clear speech.

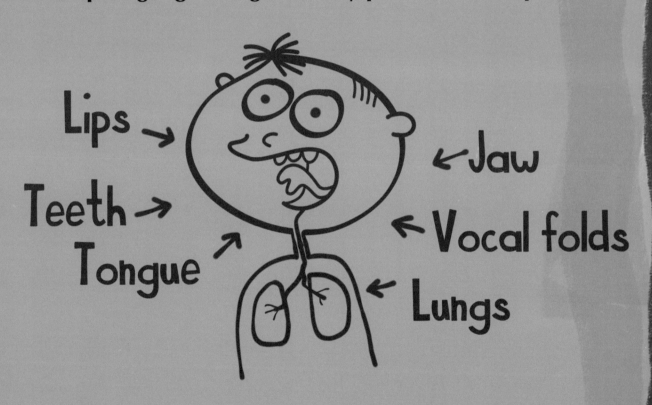

"In your case, Matthew, the speech helpers aren't always getting the right signals and they say the wrong sounds. That's why I say your mouth has a mind of its own. We will have to work hard to teach your brain and speech helper muscles to work together to make the right sounds."

Throughout the rest of the year, Matthew and Mrs. Hicks tackled one sound after another, using tongue depressors, a mirror and flashlight, a rubber mouth puppet, and hundreds of picture cards, worksheets, and games. Sometimes they even used the computer and apps on her tablet.

Matthew learned to pop his lips for /p/ and /b/ and to press his lips together for /m/. He started moving his lips out for /sh/, /ch/, and /w/ and pulling them back for /ee/. He dropped his jaw for a good /ah/ sound and rounded his lips for /oh/ and /oo/. When he put his top teeth on his bottom lip, he made great /f/ and /v/ sounds. With practice, Matthew was able to tap his tongue tip up on the gum bump behind his top teeth for /t/ and /d/, and hold it there for /n/. It took a lot of work, but finally Matthew could raise up the back of his tongue for /k/ and /g/. It made him giggle to pretend he was drinking when he said "guh, guh, guh, guh" when they practiced the /g/ sound. Matthew learned to stick out his tongue, just a little, to make the /th/ sound. Mrs. Hicks joked that making the /th/ sound was the only time in school that it was okay to stick out your tongue at a teacher.

One sound that was really tough for Matthew was /s/. Every time he tried to use it in a word, his tongue bumped up and put in a /t/ sound. Instead of "say," his mouth said, "stay." Instead of "soup," his mouth said, "stoop."

"Start with /s/, then let your tongue fall down for the next sound," explained Mrs. Hicks.
"See," thought Matthew. "Stee," said his mouth.
"So," thought Matthew. "Stow," said his mouth.
"Sing," thought Matthew. "Sting," said his mouth.

"Stop bumping up!" Matthew silently told his tongue. But he wasn't too sure that his tongue would listen. His tongue still had a mind of its own.

Mrs. Hicks was encouraging. "Don't give up, Matthew. You've tamed your lips. You've tamed your teeth and jaw. Soon you'll tame that tongue! Let's try it again. Start with /s/ and let your tongue fall down. No bumps! Say…..See……Sigh….So…Sue"

Another really hard sound was /r/. When Matthew thought "Rick's red car raced around the track," his mouth said, "Wick's wed cah waced awound the twack." By watching Mrs. Hicks and himself in the mirror, Matthew realized that he was pushing his lips out for /r/. That's what was making the /w/ sound! When Matthew learned to hold his lips back, his beginning /r/ sounds were much better.

Matthew's /r/ sounds with vowels were still not quite right, though. His mouth said "hayuh" for "hair" and "gull" for "girl" and "uth" for "earth."

"Don't worry, Matthew," Mrs. Hicks reassured him. "It can take a while to get your tongue wide and high and strong enough that it holds onto your top back teeth for /air, ar, ear, er, ire, and or/. If we can't tame your tongue for these /r/ sounds this year, we'll work on them next year.".

The practice paid off! Matthew's mouth no longer had a mind of its own. On the first day of the next school year, when his new teacher asked his name, he smiled proudly and said, "My name is Matthew!"

Find the Speech Helpers

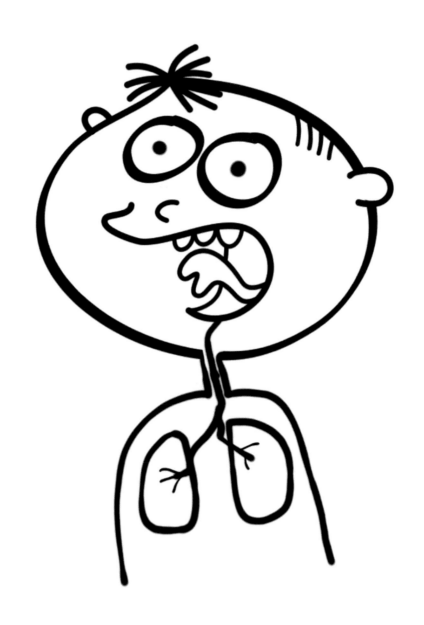

Get To Know a Speech/Language Pathologist

The students at Oliver Heckman Elementary School in Langhorne, PA, came up with a great list of questions about speech/language therapy and being a speech/language pathologist. I'll answer some of them here because maybe they are questions you've wondered about, too!

What is the name of your job?

The official name is Speech and Language Pathologist, but that's a mouthful to say, so there are other job titles that mean the same thing: speech/language clinician, speech therapist, speech teacher, and – the easiest – SLP.

Did you have to go to a special school to learn to be a speech therapist, and how long did it take?

It took six years to become an SLP. I went to our local community college for 2 years, then to a larger college for 2 years to get a Bachelor's degree, then 2 more years at the same college to get a Master's degree. I have to continue to take classes and go to workshops every year to maintain my national certification and state license.

What inspired you to become a speech therapist?

A dear uncle became very ill and lost the ability to speak. I saw how hard that was for him, and that's when I decided that I would go to college to learn to help people who have trouble communicating.

What is like working with all different kinds of kids?

It's very challenging, but I love it! I have worked with kids from 3 years old up to 21 years old. Some of my students have had lots of disabilities, and some of the kids just need help with speech, vocabulary, grammar, stuttering, reading, writing, attention, memory, or social skills.

Do you give tests and homework?

Before students can start coming to therapy, I have to give them tests to find out what skills we will be working on. These aren't tests that you can study for. Mostly, the tests involve listening, pointing to and naming pictures, and saying words and sentences. I often give homework to students who are working on improving their speech sounds, because they need to learn new muscle movements and the only way to do that is by practicing a lot.

Where do speech therapists work?

A lot of SLPs, like me, work in schools, but SLPs also work in hospitals, rehab centers, nursing homes, private offices, and even in their clients' homes. SLPs in the schools can work in the speech room, in classrooms, and even occasionally in the hallway!

How many students do you teach at one time?

Sometimes I work with just one student at a time, and sometimes I teach a whole class. Most of the time, I work with 2-4 students at a time.

What are the hardest speech sounds to teach?

The hardest, and most common, sound that kids work on in speech is /r/. Kids can usually learn the beginning /r/, as in "run," pretty quickly, but the /r/ sounds with vowels, as in "Earth, car, four, girl, and deer," are much more difficult and can take a long time to improve. Slushy-sounding /s, z, ch, sh, j/ sounds can be pretty tricky to fix, too.

What kinds of materials do you use to help students in therapy?

We use all kinds of materials: picture cards, board games, flashlights and mirrors, story books and text books, worksheets, and apps on my tablet are just a few examples.

Is it hard to understand students who have severe speech issues?

Yes, some students can be very hard to understand and some don't talk at all. I help those students communicate in other ways, such as using sign language, pictures, or augmentative communication devices that talk for them. My book, "How Katie Got a Voice (and a cool new nickname)," is about a girl who uses a communication device.

What do you do in school when you aren't with students?

Lots of paperwork!

What's your favorite part of the job?

I love working with kids! We have lots of fun together in therapy. It is a joy to watch children make progress in their speech and language.

If you have more questions about speech/language therapy, stop in and ask the SLP in your school!